P9-CMW-369

THE STORY OF
NOODLES

BY

Ying Chang Compestine

ILLUSTRATED BY

YongSheng Xuan

Holiday House / New York

"**Stop playing** with your food, boys!" scolded Mama Kang. "Remember a farmer had to sweat for every grain of rice. Pick them all up, one by one."

The three Kang boys, Pan, Ting, and Kùai, picked up the rice on the floor. Then they started cleaning up one another.

"Ho, Pan," Ting said. "You have rice in your hair."

"Oh ho, Ting," Pan answered. "You have rice in your ears."

"Oh ho ho, Ting and Pan." Kùai laughed. "You have rice in your toes."

They were still picking up the last few grains when Mama said, "It's time to get ready for bed."

When they were lying down, Kùai said to his brothers, "It takes so long to pick up all that rice. We have no time to play."

"I wish we didn't eat rice every day," said Ting.

"What else can we do?" asked Pan. "It's what everyone in China eats."

A few days later, Mama announced, "Boys, I need your help for the annual cooking contest."

"Maybe your dumplings will win again," said Ting.

"Maybe Aunt Lee's dumplings will win this year," said Pan.

"We'd better come up with something new," said Kùai.

"But your mother makes the best dumplings," said Poppa.

"And this year, we're going to make the best ones ever!" said Mama.

Early the next morning, Mama called to her family. "Let's get ready for the contest. Pan, grind some wheat in the stone grinder. Poppa, start the fire. Ting, get some water from the well. Kùai—Where is Kùai?"

"He went to feed the pigs, Mama," answered Ting.

The rest of the family pitched in to make the dumplings.

Suddenly, Kùai ran into the house. "Mama and Poppa! I can't find the black pig!"

"Mama, we'd better find our pig before it gets into the neighbor's fields," said Poppa.

"Ai yo! What am I going to do with my dumplings?" Mama asked. "You boys stay here. Roll the dumpling wrappers one at a time. Make sure they are the same size—"

Poppa dragged Mama out the door.

"Let's press the dough into a big circle and then cut it with tea cups," suggested Kùai. "They'll all be the same size."

"But Mama doesn't do it that way," Pan said.

"We can save time if we do it Kùai's way," said Ting.

They lifted the top of the stone grinder and placed it on the dough. Kùai jumped on top of the grinder. He called to his brothers, "Come on! Get on top. We need enough weight to flatten the dough!"

Ting and Pan climbed up.

BOOM! BOOM! BOOM!

The table's legs broke. The boys, the grinder, the dough, the filling, and the table flew to the floor.

"I hurt my bottom!" yelled Ting.

"Now we are in big trouble," cried Pan.

"Come on, no time to whine. Let's figure out something before Mama and Poppa come back," Kùai urged.

Soon Mama and Poppa returned with the pig. They were surprised by what they saw.

"Ai yo! What happened to my dumplings? And my table!" Mama cried.

All the dumpling dough was cut into long strips. Some strips were cooking in boiling water. Some were lying on the broken table. Others were stuck on the wall, the ceiling, and the furniture. The three boys were gathered around, eating and slurping.

"You are all in big trouble!" yelled Poppa.

"Don't be upset, Mama. We invented a new dish. Let me show you how to eat it." Pan rolled some of the long strips around the tip of his chopsticks and stuffed them into his mouth. He said, "This is called 'eating a drumstick.'"

"No, watch me!" Ting placed one end of a long strip in his mouth and sucked it in with a big slurping noise. He said, "This is called 'sucking a worm.'"

"But I know the best way, Mama and Poppa." Kùai stuffed the long strips into his mouth and bit them off with his teeth. "This is called 'cutting the grass.'"

Poppa tried not to laugh. But Mama wasn't laughing. "Now we have no time to make more dumplings. And you broke my table, too."

Kùai interrupted. "We can bring our strips to the contest."

"Yes, yes!" cheered Ting and Pan.

"Mama, I think that is all we can do. We don't have much time left," said Poppa.

Mama sighed. "All right."

To carry all the cooked strips, the Kang family used the biggest container they had, a huge new flowerpot. Together, they hauled it to the contest.

Everybody cheered when they arrived. "Oh, the Kang family! Did you bring your special dumplings? We can't wait to taste them!"

"Sorry, we didn't make dumplings this year," Mama answered sadly.

"Good for me," said Aunt Lee. She handed her dumplings to the three judges: the scholar, the king's chef, and the matchmaker.

"Han! Arr! Delicious," praised the judges. Aunt Lee smiled from ear to ear.

The judges tried many other dishes, but nothing tasted as good as Aunt Lee's dumplings.

Finally the scholar called, "The Kangs."

The Kang family carried the big pot to the table, and the whole village crowded around. "What is this? How do you eat it?"

Mama turned to her boys. "You invented this dish. You tell the judges."

The three boys lined up in front of the judges and gave perfect bows.

Kùai said, "This dish is strips made from dumpling dough."

"Can you show us how to eat the strips?" asked the matchmaker.

Each boy quickly gripped a pair of chopsticks and lined up next to the pot.

"This is called 'eating a drumstick.'" Pan wound the strips around his chopsticks and stuffed them into his mouth.

"This is called 'sucking a worm.'" Ting sucked in one with a big slurping noise.

"This is called 'cutting the grass.'" Kùai bit off the strips with his teeth.

All the children pushed closer. "Me, me! Let me try it!"

"Quiet! Quiet!" The judges silenced the crowd.

"Why did you invent a new dish?" asked the chef.

"We wanted a food that is easier to clean up after food fights," answered Kùai.

The scholar tried "eating a drumstick."

The chef tried "sucking a worm."

The matchmaker tried "cutting the grass."

The judges gathered together and talked quietly.

The crowd whispered, "They didn't say a thing after tasting the long strips. They liked Aunt Lee's dumplings the best."

Aunt Lee walked around the prize. It was covered by a large piece of red silk. She tried to figure out what the emperor had sent for the winner.

A long time seemed to pass. Finally the scholar stood up and asked, "Do these long strips have a name?"

The Kang family all looked at Kùai.

Kùai answered, "Since the strips are made of flour, we should call them *mian tiao*—flour strips."

"Good idea! Not only do they taste wonderful, but they are unusual and simple to make. I will present them to the emperor," said the chef.

"Aunt Lee's dumplings are delicious. But the emperor has already eaten many kinds of dumplings," said the scholar.

The matchmaker removed the silk from the prize and announced, "The emperor sent his best cooking table for the winner: the Kang family!"

The crowd cheered. Mama hugged her three boys.

Poppa bowed to the judges and the crowd. "Thank you! Thank you!"

Children gathered around the pot and tried "eating a drumstick," "sucking a worm," and "cutting the grass."

Before long people were eating flour strips in every part of China. From there the flour strips spread to other countries, including America, where they are called noodles.

As for the Kang family, sometimes they ate rice; other times they ate noodles.

When the boys ate rice, they no longer threw it at one
another. But when they ate noodles . . .

BOOM!

LONG-LIFE NOODLES

Makes 4 servings.

Ingredients:

$\frac{1}{2}$ pound cooked fresh or dry spaghetti noodles

For the sauce:

2 green onions, white part only, chopped

2 small cloves of garlic, peeled

$\frac{1}{2}$ cup smooth almond or peanut butter

$\frac{1}{2}$ cup coconut or soy milk

1 tablespoon lemon juice

1 tablespoon soy sauce or salt to taste

For the garnish:

$\frac{1}{4}$ cup roasted nuts

$\frac{1}{4}$ cup dried cranberries

1. With the help of an adult, chop the green onions and combine all sauce ingredients in a blender or food processor. Mix until smooth.

2. In a big bowl, toss the noodles with the sauce. Garnish with nuts and cranberries. Serve cold.

You can substitute other fruit for the cranberries. Try raisins, grapes, or fresh berries.

AUTHOR'S NOTE

Noodles originated in northern China, as early as the first century C.E. The Chinese historian Shu Hsi wrote, "Noodles and cake were mainly an invention of the common people." From China noodles spread throughout Asia.

Around the end of the thirteenth century, the Italian explorer Marco Polo introduced noodles to Italy, where they were adapted to create the first spaghetti. From Italy they spread throughout the Western world.

Rice and noodles have been the base of many meals in China. People in northern China eat more noodles than people in the south. Noodles are usually cooked in soup, fried, or eaten cold with sauce. They may be served alone or accompanied by meat, eggs, vegetables, or fruit.

Chinese children are taught to roll noodles around the tips of their chopsticks and eat them like a chicken drumstick.

It is the custom in China to make big slurping noises while eating noodles. It is believed that the louder the noise, the more delicious the noodles.

Children are allowed to bite off long noodles with their teeth. Some mothers cut the noodles with scissors before serving them to their children.

To Vinson Ming Na,
a boy who eats noodles
in many different ways!
Y. C. C.

To Zhou Er Zhuan
and Pong Lei
Y. X.

Text copyright © 2002 by Ying Chang Compestine
Illustrations copyright © 2002 by YongSheng Xuan
All Rights Reserved
Printed in the United States of America
www.holidayhouse.com
First Edition

Library of Congress Cataloging-in-Publication Data

Compestine, Ying Chang.
The story of noodles / by Ying Chang Compestine;
illustrated by YongSheng Xuan.
p. cm.
Summary: Left alone to prepare their family's prize-winning dumplings
for the annual cooking contest, the young Kang boys accidentally
invent a new dish, "mian tiao," or noodles. Includes a cultural note
and a recipe for long-life noodles.
ISBN 0-8234-1600-3
[1. Noodles—Fiction. 2. Cookery, Chinese—Fiction.
3. Family life—China— Fiction.
4. China—Fiction.] I. Xuan, YongSheng, ill. II. Title.

PZ7.C73615 Su 2002
[E]—dc21   2001059414